W. Arnold Buffum

The Tears of the Heliades

Amber as a gem

W. Arnold Buffum

The Tears of the Heliades
Amber as a gem

ISBN/EAN: 9783337361242

Printed in Europe, USA, Canada, Australia, Japan

Cover: Foto ©Andreas Hilbeck / pixelio.de

More available books at **www.hansebooks.com**

THE

TEARS OF THE HELIADES

OR

AMBER AS A GEM

BY

W. ARNOLD BUFFUM

WITH ILLUSTRATIONS

LONDON

SAMPSON LOW, MARSTON & COMPANY, LIMITED

St. Dunstan's House

FETTER LANE, FLEET STREET, E.C.

1896

CHISWICK PRESS :—CHARLES WHITTINGHAM AND CO.
TOOKS COURT, CHANCERY LANE, LONDON.

INTRODUCTION.

THE NECKLACE OF GALATEA—A MEMORIAL OF ADVENTURE IN SICILY.

It was my fortune, while pursuing some archæological studies in Italy, to assist at an excavation at Palestrina—the ancient Præneste—when, besides a mutilated *cista* of bronze and sundry objects in terra-cotta, several necklaces and fibulæ of amber and silver and amber and gold were brought to light.

The sight of these relics of a long vanished past — the intrinsic beauty of these antique ornaments, of a like period to those so carefully preserved amongst the treasures of the Gold Room of the British Museum — recalled the fact that yellow amber had a long and curious history. As the gem *par excellence* of the ancient civilized world, it was for ages the important and principal factor in the intercourse of various and widely separated peoples, thereby promoting trade ventures and commercial rivalry, and extending some of the arts of peace and culture to distant and savage lands ; while its occult powers —in which the first faint manifestations of the electric phenomena are said to have been observed—caused it to occupy the minds of savants, and its sunlike and sacred colour to stimulate the imagination of poets to account for its origin by such flights of fancy as the mythic legend which symbolized it by the tears of the Heliades, shed on the banks of Eridanus

"O'er Phaëthôn untimely dead."

So much attention has been bestowed on the natural history of amber, and so much has been written about this curious substance, that the field for any original inquiry has now been wellnigh exhausted. It is, nevertheless, my object in these pages to throw some light on the subject, to correct divers false impressions and dispel sundry illusions. The material has been gathered from the most reliable sources, and the authorities consulted are indicated in the text and footnotes. In the preparation of the work I was happily assisted, whilst on a yachting cruise in the Mediterranean in the year following the excavation at Palestrina, by an adventure in Sicily—an adventure which gave a new and, so to say, contemporary interest to my researches into the "amber-mystery," and which, therefore, I proceed to relate.

On a balmy morning in February our good yacht came in sight of the snowy pyramid of Ætna, uprising from its fringe of green in silent majesty, dazzling-white, the multitudinous spires and domes of Aci Reale—a city set on lofty lava hills —glistening in the foreground. It was my desire to make the ascent of the mountain from this point, and we landed without difficulty in the bay of Trezza, on the identical spot, perchance, chosen by Ulysses and his companions for disembarking from their hollow ship when, after weary wanderings over the stormy deep, they ventured, high of heart, on a visit to the Cyclops. This, at all events, I felt confident, was the Portus Ulyssis of Virgil :

" Portus ab accessu ventorum immotus, et ingens
  Ipse ; sed horrificis juxta tonat Ætna ruinis—" [1]

which opinion was confirmed by the sight of a cave, beyond the mead of golden asphodel, "on the border near to the sea," as described by Homer,[2] and by the presence in the bay of the dark-brown rocks which the monster hurled after the defiant Odysseus.

The havoc wrought by Ætna along this

---

[1] " Æn." iii. 570.

[2] " The Odyssey of Homer." Done into English prose by S. H. Butcher, M.A., and A. Lang, M.A., ix. 157-189.

coast is manifest from Taormina to Catania.
Here, at Trezza, volcanic tufa is scattered
in all directions; the ground we tread on is
a bed of cinders, and from the tiny, scoria-
scorched beach where I stood, waving
farewells to my friends and the good yacht,
huge blocks of black lava jut far out
into the sea, lending an aspect of rugged
desolation to the scene. But beauty lingers
in the lap of ruin, and gems with wild
flowers "the hillside that fronts the dawn."

" Laurel, and cypress tall, and ivy dun,
And vines of sumptuous fruitage, all are there :
And a cold spring that pine-clad Ætna flings
Down from the white snow's midst, a draught for
    gods." [1]

----

[1] "Theocritus." Translated into English verse by
C. S. Calverley. Idyll XI.

A carriage not being readily obtainable, I climbed the steep and stony road that leads from the hamlet of Trezza to Aci Reale, a road unsightly and charmless, for, grey, dusty, and uneven, it runs mostly between high walls built of dreariest lava, the more annoying as one knows they hide from view all that is grateful to the northern eye : *e.g.,* vineyards of trellised and hanging vines and orchards, where the orange, the lemon, the pomegranate and the mulberry vie with the almond, the olive, the date-palm and the nespolo for the prize of luxuriance. Half-way up, however, a turn in the lane restored to view the mountain,

" . . . in the broad glare
Of the hot noon, without a shade,"

and the classic shore, with its turquoise and violet bays and patches of shining yellow beach, where Pindar wandered, watching the waves, and where, just beyond the legendary rocks, rose the bold basaltic cliff and feudal fortress of Aci Castello— the scene of many a sanguinary conflict and of one heroic, memorable defence—off which a solitary fishing boat with reddish-brown and lemon-coloured sails was visible, looking like a moth-butterfly, skimming the seas with expanded wings.

It was *un giorno di festa* and, as the bells at Aci rang out a joyous peal in honour of the day, a troop of gleeful children, with flowers and wreaths in their hands, came singing down the road on the way to some rural jollity.

BAY OF TREZZA—THE CYCLOPEAN ROCKS—ACI CASTELLO.

But who is this ?   The nymph Galatea, by all that's wonderful !

As I pause, the gates of one of these inclosed orchards are thrown wide, and from the shadowy depths of luxuriant green I see approaching one of those gaily-painted, two-wheeled *carrette*, so common in Southern Italy and Sicily, driven by a lithe and comely maiden in the pretty gala costume of the well-to-do peasants of this part of the island.   Around her throat there hung a necklace of sparkling gems, partially hidden by a silken scarf or *manto*, and roseate blossoms of the almond tree, now in full bloom, bedecked her dusky hair.   A fitting background to this radiant vision was the *duenna*, seated in the rear of the vehicle, with face of bronze as seamy and forbidding as the lava walls that guard the orchard's tempting and luscious fruit.

Summoning up my best Italian, I begged this nymph to drive me to the town, to which request, "with a sweet modesty," she assented. Not, however, before I distinctly heard the voice of the dragon muttering between her teeth, by way of remonstrance, "*forestiere, forestiere,*"[1] in much the same agreeable tone one sometimes hears its equivalent uttered in more enlightened lands.

On the way up the rugged hill the maiden told me Ætna—or "Mongibello," as she termed it in the Saracenic-Sicilian dialect

---

[1] Foreigner, foreigner.

— had recently exhibited exceptional activity:

"Shot balls of fire and rolled forth molten rocks."

Whilst she spoke, the gems in her necklace flashed in the sunlight, showing colour-shades ranging from faint blue to deepest azure, and from pale rose to intense, pigeon-blood, ruby red. The varied and lustrous hues, here blended in lavish beauty, drew from me involuntary expressions of admiration, and I asked if the stones were found in Sicily.

"Si, Signore," responded the nymph, "this necklace is of amber."

"Amber!" I exclaimed, "amber?"

"Si, Signore," she answered, "*ambra di Sicilia.*"

"Amber of Sicily; impossible!" I said.

" Amber, as everyone knows, is yellow :—
these stones are red, green, orange, violet;
and here is a blue one, the colour of the
sky :—*un pezzo di cielo caduto in terra !*"

" Nevertheless," replied Galatea, smiling
at my incredulity, " this is Sicilian amber;
un prodotto dell' Isola—found here on these
shores—and genuine amber."

" But the colours, the colours!" I cried :
" Whence came these lovely and fluorescent hues ?"

" That," said the maiden, with reverent
gesture, " one must ask of the *buon Dio.*
But the colours are normal—these are
pristine hues."

" They are hues, then, of the primeval
world," I said—" the imprisoned colour-
shades of an earlier and more exuberant

clime—and it seems strange so peerless a gem should be unknown in other lands, amongst the glittering throng."

" Not for them only, as they are wont to deem, is beauty beautiful," responded the nymph, quoting, with slight variations, the Sicilian poet Theocritus. " Besides," she added, " you must know that, with colours like these, amber is scarce even in Sicily."

" How does that happen ?" I inquired.

" *Chi lo sa?* Formerly it was abundant, but of late little is found."

" Then perhaps you will sell me this necklace?" I said, eager to possess so incomparable a treasure.

" No, no, I cannot part with it," replied Galatea.

" But I will pay a good price for it."

" *Non importa,*" she said, " I will not sell it: it is an heirloom in the family—a talisman that has brought us good luck. If the signore would like a necklace of this sort, he must buy it of the *negociante* in Catania."

In a few minutes we arrived in the Piazza del Duomo of Aci Reale where, finding my efforts to purchase the magical necklace unavailing, I alighted at the albergo dell' Aurora, and thanking Galatea for her courtesy, and rewarding the duenna, I bade them *addio.*

Ambra di Sicilia! Yes, she had said it! Amber of Sicily—gem of the Sicilian sea!

*   *   *   *   *

I made the ascent of Ætna and the *giro*

of the island, and before leaving Sicily, succeeded in collecting numerous specimens, rivalling, in the soft splendour and beauty of their hues, the necklace of Galatea.

The coloured plate in the frontispiece has been executed with care, but it has been found impossible to reproduce the exquisite colour-shades of Sicilian amber, which in vivacity surpass those of the opal, and the plate conveys only a faint notion of this lovely and curious gem.

W. A. B.

VENICE, *September*, 1896.

CONTENTS.

CHAPTER III.

CHAPTER IV.

ILLUSTRATIONS.

THE

TEARS OF THE HELIADES;

OR, AMBER AS A GEM.

CHAPTER I.

The Heliades' legend—Varieties—Ambra di Sicilia
—Its properties and charm—Ornaments of other days
—A fashionable gem—Was it known to the ancients?
—Phœnician amber merchants—Tales for the credulous—The mythical Elektrides and the river Po.

THE Greek legend of the Heliades, of
which both Hyginus and Ovid have given
elaborate versions, recounts the adventures
and death of Phaëthôn, the favourite child
of the Sun-god Hêlios, in his rash attempt
to drive the horses harnessed to the chariot

of the sun which, at his solicitation, his
father had entrusted to him for a day.
Seized with dizziness and terror on the
height, Phaëthôn, losing all control of the
wild steeds, approached too near the earth
and set it on fire.   At the earnest entreaty
of the goddess Earth, who feared to be
consumed, Jupiter launched a thunderbolt
at Phaëthôn, who forthwith fell into the
Eridanus.   The naiads of the stream buried
the body on the shore, to which it had been
washed by the foaming waves.   His sisters,
the Heliades—Aegle, Dioxippê, Lampetiê,
Phaëthusa, and the rest—accompanied by
their mother, the beauteous Klymenê, a
daughter of Oceanus, found at last the
tomb of their brother ; and remaining beside
it, weeping bitterly, they became rooted to

the spot and, for assisting Phaëthôn in yoking the steeds to the chariot and encouraging his adventure, were changed into trees from whose branches tears continually fall. These, Ovid adds, are hardened by the heat of the sun and become amber, which the beaming river receives and sends to the Roman ladies to adorn their persons.

Milton refers to the same myth in the lines :

" Him the thunderer hurled
From the empyrean headlong to the gulf
Of the half-parched Eridanus, where weep
Even now the sister trees their amber tears
O'er Phaëthôn, untimely dead."

Such is the fanciful, but, nevertheless, faithful account, current amongst the ancient Greeks, of the derivation of amber from the resin of trees. To make it scientifically accurate and up to date, it is only necessary to add that amber is the resin of an extinct *pinus*, called by Prof. Göppert *pinites succinifer*, which flourished in the lower Tertiary Period. This resin has become fossilized in the earth, and is a substance which cannot be successfully imitated or falsified.[1]

The popular idea of amber is founded

---

[1] Amber is very light, having a specific gravity of 1·o8 to 1·10. The diamond is pure carbon; amber is 81 per cent. carbon. Chemical analysis shows that in 100 grammes of amber there are:

Carbon	. 81
Hydrogen .	7·30
Oxygen .	6·75

And traces of clay, alumina, and silica, amounting to about 5 grammes.

solely on a knowledge of the yellow
variety from the Baltic, which, it is generally believed, has supplied, from time
immemorial, the markets of the world.
Other sources have been little known, and
the varieties they afford are seldom met
with. But amber, "distilled by pines that
were dead before the days of Adam,"
is widely distributed over the northern
portion of the earth, and is found also in
Roumania, on the Lower Danube, and in
Sicily in stinted measure, but of colours
proportionately rare. Roumanian, German,
and Sicilian amber are nearly related.
They differ, however, in colour and "fire,"
just as diamonds differ in lustre and
"water." But the peculiar, distinctive
quality of Sicilian amber, that which dis-

tinguishes it from its congeners and gives
it its indescribable charm and expression,
is its *fluorescence*—"that property which
some transparent bodies have of producing
at their surface, or within their substance,
light different in colour from the mass of
the material, as when green crystals of
fluor-spar afford blue reflections. This
curious property is due not to the difference in the colour of a distinct surface
layer, but to the power which the substance
has of modifying the light incident upon
it." Thus, in my collection specimens
may be seen which show sapphire blue,
pale rose, violet, and brilliant ruby hues—
the actual colour of the pieces being straw-
yellow and faint olive-green.

Roumanian amber is usually of a dark-brown hue, of a rich and subdued beauty, with shining gold and silver flecks and bluish and greenish tints. German amber is yellow in various shades, sometimes running into white or brown, but all the colours in the prismatic spectrum are met with in the Sicilian variety. From the sober grey of early dawn to the burning crimson that sets the clouds aflame at evening after sunset, there are few tints the sunbeams paint through summer days that have not been transfused, as if by Ætna's fires, and blended in Trinacria's lustrous and pellucid sun-stone. In this opulence of hues Sicilian amber is matchless among gems:

. . . "divinely bright,
Like radiant Hesper o'er the gems of night;"

and, while any glamour is left in colour, it cannot fail to produce those pleasing effects which result from harmonious combinations and agreeable contrasts.

The ancient writers make no reference to Sicilian amber, and I have been unable to find any direct mention of it before A.D. 1639.[1] Diodorus (Siculus), who was born on the island at Agyrium, now S. Filippo d'Agiro, near to places which furnish it in considerable quantities—where I myself have picked it up from the surface of the ground—makes no allusion to it. He declares the Greek legend about Phaëthôn and the metamorphosis of the tears of the Heliades into amber as they dropped into

---

[1] Carrera, "Memorie Storiche di Catania, 1639."

the Eridanus to be fable, and assures us that this mineral, which in his day was a fashionable gem in great request, is only to be found on the shores of the island of Basilia [1] " beyond Gallia, opposite Scythia," whence, he says, it was carried to the neighbouring continent by the native inhabitants, and in this way reached the Mediterranean through Gaul. [2]

The absolute silence of the ancient writers lends colour to the supposition that the Sicilian variety was unknown to the

---

[1] This name is taken from the writings of Pytheas of Massilia, who, in the fourth century B.C. made a voyage to the North in search, it is supposed, of the amber-land. Basilia may refer to the Frisian island Ameland, or possibly to Jutland.

[2] Diodorus, v. 23.

ancients; but Sir A. Wollaston Franks,[1] of the British Museum, and some Continental authorities, are inclined to the opinion that the amber employed in ornaments discovered in Italo-Greek and Etruscan tombs was derived from Sicily. The amber seen in these ornaments is almost always of a dark-red hue, wholly unlike the normal colour of Baltic amber and, at the same time, readily distinguishable from the red amber found in Sicily at the present day. But the colour, in this case, affords no indication as to the origin of the material. Amber, from whatever source it comes, after being cut and polished, is easily affected by atmospheric

---

[1] Franks, "Cong. Int. Archeol. Prehist. Buda-Pest," 1876, 433.

and other influences [1] which tend to darken
its colour, impair its quality, and produce
the well-known *patina* observed in old
German amber beads and art objects of
fifteenth and sixteenth-century workman-
ship. These changes begin at the surface,
and less than a century is sufficient to turn
even golden-yellow amber to a dark, rust-
coloured red. Whether the ornaments
discovered in these ancient tombs are of
German or Italian amber cannot, therefore, be determined by their colour as it
meets the eye — this being simply the
effect of age and external influences—
and the author of these pages, greatly

---

[1] Amber ornaments deposited in tombs are, doubtless, affected by chemical processes acting within the
soil.

interested in the question, "was Sicilian amber known to the ancients?" has, accordingly, cut up sundry antique amber amulets, whorls, etc., and found, after removing the exterior part, a kernel, showing the normal and unaffected hue of the substance, and he has no hesitation in saying that some of these pre-historic amulets and whorls were unmistakably of the Sicilian variety.

Indeed, the opinion has gained ground in recent years, that Sicilian amber—not the amber of the Baltic—first attracted the attention of the ancient civilized world. Amber, it is now known, is a product of a former geological epoch, and the deposits in Sicily must, therefore, have existed in its soil for long ages. Is it to be supposed that in ancient times—in the golden days of Assyria and primitive and heroic Greece —the destructive processes of denudation had not yet uncovered it ? Is it possible that the mountain-torrents had not then washed it out of the primary strata in which it was deposited in the *miocene* age ? Or can it be that the amber of Sicily was in use amongst the ancients while the place of its origin remained to them unknown ?

Nicias, according to Pliny,[1] says that in Egypt amber was called *sakal* and, as *sakal* is not an Egyptian word, it has long been suspected that it is the name originally adopted with the amber which the

---

[1] Pliny, "Nat. Hist." xxxvii. 11, 36.

Egyptians obtained from the *Sikeli* (the Sicilians), a powerful and warlike race, established on the East coast of the island of Trinacria, before the dawn of history, in full control of the region which has since yielded thousands of pounds of "loveliest amber." The peoples of the Mediterranean countries had commercial relations with one another from the earliest time, though piracy, rapine and kidnapping, no doubt, played an important part in early trade ventures, as we may see by the thrilling account in the Odyssey, of an attack on the villages and towns of the Delta.

" By Egypt's silver flood our ships we moor ;
Our spies commission'd straight the coast explore ;
But, impotent of mind, with lawless will
The country ravage, and the natives kill.

The spreading clamour to their city flies,
And horse and foot in mingled tumult rise.

     *   *   *   *

Jove thunder'd on their side : our guilty head
We turn'd to flight."

Raids of this sort, doubtless, were made on Sicily, and victorious Egyptian pirates, or, perhaps, honest traders or warriors, may have carried away with them Sicily's lovely amber under the name of *sakal.*

Sicily,[1] it is well known, has been the theatre of the most formidable convulsions ; and even in comparatively recent years

---

[1] In a former period Sicily was connected with Africa on the one hand and with Italy on the other, the land area being then lifted up more than two thousand feet, while the area of the Mediterranean Sea was very greatly reduced. Sicily, Malta, and Crete are said to be the higher portions of a continent now submerged.

earthquakes and volcanic eruptions have changed the aspect of whole districts. The effect of phenomena of this character on the productiveness of the deposits in the soil cannot, of course, be determined ; but it may safely be presumed that Sicily was not without amber in the olden time, and that the amber traders, those at any rate who furnished the Greeks, did obtain supplies from this source. But, as their object was to sell their wares at the highest prices, it is easy to see that they had an interest in keeping the secret of the existence in Trinacria of this costly sun-stone to themselves. That the Phœnicians knew how to guard their trade secrets is shown by the well-known story of the Phœnician ship-master who, when followed by a Roman on one occasion, purposely steered his vessel upon a shoal, and brought about the wreck of his own and his pursuer's ship rather than allow the Roman to learn the secret of his route. For this he was rewarded by the State.[1]

" The Phœnician amber merchants long before the time of Homer," says the eminent antiquarian Voss,[2] " related to the credulous

---

[1] Strabo, iii., c. v., s. ii.

[2] I have translated this passage from the learned and interesting essay, " Der Bernstein in Ostpreussen," Berlin, 1868, by Dr. Wilhelm Runge, who informs me that it is taken from a brochure entitled, " Alte Welt-kunde " (Ancient Geography) printed in Roman characters, comprising thirty-seven pages, and preceded by a map, handsomely engraved on copper, bearing the title, " Hesiod's World Table, by J. H. Voss, engraved by T. Goetz, Weimar, 1804." Voss had

that in the north-western part of Hesiod's disk of the earth, the river Eridanus, descending from the high Rhipæan mountains (the Alps), falls into the ocean, and at its mouth certain trees, under the influence of the hot sun gliding past, exude amber, called by them *elektron*, or sun-stone. But it was a part of the Phœnician State policy, from the earliest times to the fall of Carthage, to spread a veil over the western lands beyond Sicily by means of fables, pretended ignorance, violence and State treaties. Hence they gave the Greeks the following mysterious account of the very ancient

---

previously translated Homer, was the author of a "Commentary on Virgil's Poems," and the "Mythological Letters," and had made wide researches in ancient history and geography.

trading track to Tartessus and the north-west of Europe, the source of tin and amber, which they reached at a much earlier period than the ivory coast in the west of Africa.

' Passing behind Trinacria (Sicily) one comes to the mouth of the ocean which encircles the whole earth : one steers past Atlas on the left—the pillar of the vaulted sky—together with the gate of the Sun and the happy elysium, leaving to the right, on the Cimmerian strand, the portals of the nether world and the sources of the ocean in a silver rock sustaining the heavens : then, amidst incredible dangers, one follows the dark shore to the isles of tin, and to the stream Eridanus, in which the costly sun-stone, *elektron*, falls in drops from certain resinous trees, by reason of the glowing heat of Helios sailing back to Colchis.'

"For still greater security, the Phœni-cians populated the entrance to the ocean

with uninviting chimeras, and as enlighten-
ment on this point increased, the terrors on
the other side (in accordance with the then
prevailing notions) were redoubled.   Must
not the Phœnicians, who had founded the
colony of Gadeira still earlier than Utica
at the entrance to the terrible ocean, have
smiled in listening to the credulous strains
of the Homers and Hesiods, if indeed their
love of the useful allowed them to notice
such trifles as these ?"

The amber of Sicily is found on the
eastern and south-eastern coasts, and
sparsely in almost all the adjacent districts,
and it is met with in the middle of the island,
near the foot of the Central Mountains,
mostly in small pieces, but sometimes the
size of an orange, on the surface of the

ground, in the furrows of freshly ploughed fields, and in the stone-strewn *fiumari*, beds of streams left dry. In the spring and autumn, after heavy rains, which turn the countless mountain rivulets into torrents, and wash the amber out of the clayey soil, it is borne by brooks and streamlets to the great rivers, the Simeto and the Salso, which carry it on to the sea, the waves throwing it upon the shore near the mouths of these rivers, not far from Catania and Licata. At Calascibetta and at Castrogiovanni—the Enna of the ancients, "the umbilicus of Sicily," the scene of the worship of Demeter and the rape of Persephone—pieces of fluorescent amber, according to the reports of Hoffmann and others, have been discovered in a brownish-grey, porous sandstone, mixed with lignite. These layers have been examined by Maravigna and Gemmellaro, who recognized the rocks as belonging to tertiary formations.

A stratum of marl and slate near Caltanisetta, containing amber, has also been determined by Notturno to belong to the *Miocene.* Amber is found, too, at Leonforte and at S. Filippo d'Agiro, where Diodorus was born ; in the territories of the two Petralia, near Monte Salvatore, and on the shores of Terranova, Scicli, Pozzallo, Spaccaforno, and in the Val di Noto, near Ragusa. The nodules almost invariably have well-rounded forms, the skin, generally the colour of iron-rust, being smooth and thin, which goes to show that for a

long time they have been subjected to
the action of water, and rolled about over
sandy surfaces. The pieces differ greatly
in value. Many of them are worthless,
but the flawless ones with rare and irides-
cent hues, though no bigger than a walnut,
sometimes bring forty or fifty pounds
sterling each. The peasants eagerly seek
for the precious mineral after every storm,
knowing well the high price it commands,
but thus far no organized or adequate
attempts have been made to dig for it.[1]

---

[1] In the excavations undertaken by the Prussian
government in Samland, a district of East Prussia on
the Baltic, a few years since, amber-bearing layers
were met with below the marl and greensand formations: *i.e.*, from sixty to eighty feet below the surface
of the ground, and they occur in the shore declivities

The widespread, isolated, and "nestwise" surface deposits, however, have greatly diminished in recent years, in some dry seasons hardly any choice pieces being found on the island, and it would not be surprising if these deposits were to cease, and the amber of Sicily to disappear.

In his amusing letters from Sicily, published in 1770, Patrick Brydone mentions that at the mouth of the Giarretta, formerly the Symæthus, which falls into the Mediterranean near the ruins of ancient Morgantium, great quantities of fine amber are thrown up, which at Catania finds a ready sale at high prices, when carved

---

at much greater depths. It is believed that valuable amber-bearing layers exist in the soil of Sicily, which can only be reached by the miner's shaft.

into crosses, beads, figures of saints, etc. This statement is interesting, as it enables us to note the changes which a century has here brought about—the amber found at the mouth of the Giarretta at the present day being limited to a few nodules only. Brydone and his companions seem to have been much impressed with this material, some of which contained insects. They bought several amber figures, and were entertained by the ingenuity of an artist who had contrived to leave embedded in the substance a large fly, with expanded wings, hovering just over the head of a saint, as the artist remarked, "to represent *Lo Spirito Santo* descending upon him."

Goethe mentions a collection of Sicilian

amber seen by him towards the end of last century at Catania, where the Museo Biscari was rich in *objets d'art* in this substance; and Sestini says amber was held in such esteem that a necklace of large beads was always among the presents given by parents to a daughter on her marriage.

Italy no longer produces amber in marketable quantities, but small pieces are picked up in the Transpadane districts and the Emilia. In the olden time it was said to be found on the Padus (the Po), the chief river of Northern Italy, whose name came from the pine-trees (in Celtic, *padi*), which grew upon its banks. The neighbourhood of the Padus, it is believed, was the scene of the Heliades' legend, and near the mouths of this abounding stream, which

Virgil terms "*fluviorum rex Eridanus,*"[1]
"the ocean wave of the Adriatic shore"
encircled the Elektrides, or Amber Islands
of the Greeks; and these, it has been
suggested, may have been the actual Eu-
ganean Mountains which now form many
isolated groups in the plains of Padua.
The constant deposit of sediment brought
down by the river, which has its sources in
the glaciers of the Alps, and frequently
overflows its banks, has, it is thought, in
the lapse of time, united these islands to
one another and to the continent, and in
this way buried the precious amber-masses
out of sight. In the same manner the oozy
Po has created a vast delta along the

---

[1] "Georg." i. 482.

Venetian coast, and silted up the harbours of Ravenna and ancient Hadria, or Hatria, the Etruscan seaport which gave its name to the Adriatic as well as to the *atrium*, or court of Roman houses.   Ravenna, which Augustus made one of the principal stations of the Roman fleet, was formerly situated directly on the sea, but now lies six or seven miles inland; while Hatria, where Etruscan ships rode at anchor, is fifteen or sixteen miles distant from the Adriatic shore.

CHAPTER II.

THE yellow amber of commerce, now largely relegated to the service of Smoke, where it is adored in a pipe, or peradventure banished to oriental lands, where, as odorous incense, it ascends continually in Buddhist temples or Mohammedan mosques for the delectation of devout worshippers, has shed its lustre on the charms of beauty and added splendour to the courts of kings. For a very long period it was the chief article of traffic between the primitive races of Western and Northern Europe and the cultivated nations of Western Asia, as well as the countries bordering on the Mediterranean.

The beginning of the overland trade in yellow amber is lost in the mists of pre-historic times, but as we know that some simple trade, limited to a few articles, was carried on as early as the Stone Age,[1] we may fairly presume that this commodity, at a remote period, found its way to distant lands, Assyria and beyond, having passed, at first, from hand to hand and from tribe

---

[1] Among the remains of the Stone Age in Europe, beautifully wrought jade axes have been discovered, jade being a material produced only in China and the farthest East.

to tribe, by way of barter, until it reached the shores of the Euxine, where the Scythians and Cimmerians had settlements, and whence it was distributed by caravans or Phœnician ships.

Amber ornaments are found in the prehistoric remains of Egypt, Greece, Italy, and other lands, rare and costly examples of which enrich the private cabinets and public museums of the world. Considering the delicate and fragile nature of the substance, it might be supposed that these primordial creations of art would long since have crumbled to dust and wholly disappeared; but, as may be seen, the amber ornaments now in the British Museum and in my own collection, have escaped the ravages of time almost as completely as the terra-cotta vases, the ivories, or even the bronze and silver bowls unearthed at Mykenæ and Cyprus.

Amber ornaments occur, too, in the tumuli of the Stone Age in Britain and in almost every country of Europe, and they appear in the remains of the Lake-dwellers of Switzerland and France belonging to the same period. This general and extended use of the material shows how highly it was prized, and affords another and a striking proof of the early development of man's æsthetic sense, from which have sprung the arts and refinements of modern society.

It would seem, from a cuneiform inscription by a king of Nineveh on a broken obelisk, translated by Professor J. Oppert, one of the ablest Assyriologists, that very early commercial relations existed between Assyria and the north of Europe. Prof. Oppert[1] translates the inscription of this ancient monarch :

"In the sea of changeable winds (*i.e.*, the Persian Gulf)

his merchants fished for pearls ;

in the sea where the North star culminates (*i.e.*, the Baltic)

they fished for yellow amber."

Doubts, it is true, have been thrown upon the correctness of this rendering. But when were scholars known to agree?

Lenormant[2] points out the road, in-

---

[1] "L'Ambre Jaune chez les Assyriens," par J. Oppert.

[2] M. François Lenormant, in "The Contemporary Review," for September, 1878.

dicated by Herodotus, which led from ancient Olbia to the north, and was taken by the Greeks of the Milesian colonies established on the Euxine, when going in quest of the amber of the Baltic. " This road skirted the foot of the Carpathians, crossed Silesia and the Duchy of Posen, thus directly reaching Pomerania and thence Jutland, and it is marked along its whole extent by discoveries of Greek coins of the most ancient style. It is a road pointed out by nature itself, and which must have been taken from extremely remote times by several migratory peoples. Of late years remarkable traces have been found, calculated to convince us that it had been frequented by numerous traders long before the time of the Milesians of Olbia.

We are therefore led by probability to connect with the commerce that took this road those great deposits of bronze weapons and utensils found in the lakes of Switzerland, and to ascribe to it a decisive influence on the bronze age of the North."

Later, when Rome held the provinces on the Danube, amber was brought by this same route to the Roman fortress-towns, where it passed out of the hands of its semi-barbarous owners into those of their masters. By a different and less-known route amber was sent to the North Sea by the Oder and the Elbe, then it reached the Rhine, and, conveyed up this stream and down the Rhone, it came to the hands of the traders at Massilia. A direct road from Liguria to the North Sea crossed the Alps by the Little St. Bernard, thus gaining the valley of the Aar, and thence the Rhine. Other roads led north-ward from ancient Hatria, near the mouth of the Po, and the valuable trade in amber over some of these roads continued in a flourishing condition, increasing in volume and importance, long after the discovery of sea-routes to the amber-land by the Phœnicians.

Herodotus[1] does "not allow that there is any river, to which the barbarians give the name of Eridanus, emptying itself into the northern sea, whence (as the tale goes) amber is procured;" nor does he know of

---

[1] Herod. iii. 115.

any islands called Cassiterides, whence comes tin ;—" Nevertheless," he says, "amber and tin do certainly come to us from the ends of the earth." Amber and tin, no doubt, were the commodities which first led the ancients to take an interest in the north and west of Europe, and it is interesting to note that civilization was promoted and extended through the commerce which sprung up in this merchandise. Amber was required for ornament, and tin was in great request for the manufacture of bronze—which is an alloy of tin and copper. In the Bronze Age it is not probable that Sicily, Italy, and the Danube furnished enough amber to satisfy the demand, or that the tin mines of Tuscany, or those of Spain and Brittany, from which the Etruscans and the Phœnicians obtained supplies, yielded the metal in sufficient quantities for the purposes of commerce.

The Phœnicians, the great merchants of antiquity, a bold, seafaring race, who had the whole carrying trade of the Ægean and the Mediterranean in their hands, even " in those remote days when the Greeks were still waiting to receive the elements of their culture from the more civilized East" [1] must, therefore, have seized upon the opportunity for profitable trade, created by the demand for these important products.   In searching for them the adventurous mariners of Tyre and Sidon, having regard to the difficulties surrounding the overland trade, pushed

[1] See Prof. A. H. Sayce, "The Phœnicians in Greece."—"Contemporary Review," December, 1878.

their voyages beyond the pillars that held up the vaulted sky, past the dread portals of the nether world, to brave the terrors of that unknown sea, where only their bright-winged fancies and their hopes of coveted wealth had gone before them. The date of this romantic and daring achievement is uncertain ; but there are abundant reasons for believing that more than a thousand years before our era the Phœnicians had ventured into the Atlantic, had visited Britain for tin, and the shores of Germany for amber, carrying with them some of the civilization and civilizing influences then existing on the borders of the Mediterranean.[1] These expeditions, so far as we

---

[1] See Sir John Lubbock, "Prehistoric Times," 5th ed. p. 74. Sir John Lubbock finds strong objec-

know, were the first *ocean* voyages ever made by man.   Milton's picture of a ship of Tarsus :

> ". . . bound for th' isles
> Of Javan or Gadire,
> With all her bravery on and tackle trim,
> Sails filled and streamers waving ;
> *An amber scent of odorous perfume*
> Her harbinger—"

recalls one of these primeval maritime enterprises.

---

tions to Professor Nilsson's opinion that the Bronze Age civilization in the North of Europe was due to the influence of Phœnician commerce.   But he calls attention to Professor Nilsson's statements that the Phœnicians had settlements far up on the northern shores of Norway where, it is pointed out, Baal, the god of the Phœnicians, has left traces of his worship in many Scandinavian localities ; *i.e.*, the Baltic, the Great and Little Belt, Belteberga, Balestranden, etc.   "The festival of Baal, or Balder,

The Greeks called amber ἤλεκτρον, *elek-tron*,[1] a name they probably adopted with the substance from the Phœnicians, as they

---

according to Professor Nilsson, was celebrated on midsummer's night in Scania and far up into Norway almost to the Loffoden Islands, until within a recent period. A wood fire was made upon a hill or mountain, and the people of the neighbourhood gathered together in order, like Baal's prophets of old, to dance round, shouting and singing. This Midsummer's Night fire has even retained, in some parts, the ancient name of 'Baldersbal' or 'Balder's fire.' L. v. Buch long ago suggested that this custom could not have originated in a country where at midsummer the sun is never lost sight of, and where, consequently, the smoke only, not the fire, is visible."

[1] *El ek* in Arabic, and perhaps in Phœnician, signifies "the resin." Scholars derive *elektron* from one of the Homeric names of the Sun-god, *Elektôr*, and this is referred by Professor Curtius to a root, *ark*, "to shine."

adopted from the same source the names
of other articles of luxury, the letters of the
alphabet, and their early culture ; and from
elektron, in which the earliest manifestations
of the electric phenomena were observed,
is derived our word "electricity." The
Egyptians engraved on it the images of
their deities, and it is believed to have
formed one of the four aromas employed in
the Tabernacle according to the prescrip-
tions of Moses. The Romans named it *suc-
cinum*, from *succus* (juice), and also styled
it *lapis ardens*. For the same reason the
Germans termed it *Bernstein*, both names
signifying a stone that burns ; and Tacitus [1]
states that the Æstyans, who gathered it on

---

[1] "Germania," 45.

the Baltic coast, called it *gless*, whence comes
" glass."

Fashion, which "shifts like the sands,
the sport of every wind," was for once
constant, and amber maintained its high
value in the ancient civilized world—leaving
out of account brief periods of neglect—to
fall into disuse in the Middle Ages. With
the artists of the Revival, however, it was
a favourite material, and the National
Museums at Florence, Naples, Palermo,
and Vienna, the Grüne Gewölbe at Dres-
den, the Industrial Museum at Berlin, the
Louvre and the Musée Cluny in Paris, contain Renaissance amber objects; *e.g.*, jewel-
caskets, reliquarii, vases, cassette, crucifixes,
statuettes, candelabra, drinking cups, etc.
The South Kensington Museum has a few

objects of seventeenth century workman-
ship, and my own collection is rich in
masterpieces of fifteenth and sixteenth
century art in this substance. In these
treasures we possess some of the finest
examples of art as applied to industry.

It has, I know, been suggested that our
regard for amber is due to a hereditary
instinct ; that it is a survival of an ancient
superstition which considered the mineral
of celestial origin—as Sun-stuff! This view
has been ably maintained by Dr. F. A.
Paley [1] in an article entitled " Gold Worship
in its Relation to Sun Worship," in which
he shows that amber and gold were super-
stitiously valued for their yellow colour,

---

[1] See "Contemporary Review," August, 1884.

AMBER JEWEL CASKET.

because they were of the same colour and possibly of the same divine material as the sun; and he himself was evidently under the influence of this "hereditary passion," for he says he has often thought that amber is one of " the objects which please most by an indefinable gracefulness of colour, a subdued lustre that satisfies without dazzling the eye."

Sun-worship, no doubt, was widespread if not universal in ancient times. The Phœnicians brought it with them from the Orient when they came to the Mediterranean, and their temples built to Baal were temples of the sun. The Greeks and Romans had the same worship. It would be strange, therefore, if amber, which is more sun-like than any gem distilled in

Nature's great alembic, should have failed to excite the admiration of sun-worshipping man. When he saw that it was instinct with life, that—as the philosopher Thales of Miletus declared 600 years before our era—"it had a soul," these "clots of sunshine" must have had for him an irresistible attraction, accompanied, it may be, by a superstitious regard. The likeness of amber to the sun was, at any rate, clearly familiar to the Greeks, for Homer[1] describes the necklace Eurimachus gives to Penelope as,

"Golden, set with amber, like the radiant sun!"

Amber is the only gem Homer mentions in his minute descriptions of the jewelry and art-wares of ancient times; and it is

---

[1] "Odyssey," xviii. 296.

not difficult to believe that this magic stone was prized by the *grandes dames* of the court of Agamemnon and by the ladies of Argos and Mykenæ and tower-engirded Thebes, as a jewel fit to serve as a personal ornament, to adorn their shoulders and bedeck their hair withal. Amber is named three times in the "Odyssey,"[1] and as regards the triple-gemmed earrings of Juno ("Il." xiv. 183) :

> "Fair beaming pendants tremble in her ears,
> Each seems illumined with a triple star ;"

and ("Od." xviii. 298) :

> "Earrings bright
> With triple stars that cast a trembling light ;"

there is every reason for the opinion that the bard was here also referring to amber.

---

[1] "Odyssey," iv. 73 ; xv. 460 ; xviii. 296.

E

Homer [1] speaks of amber as employed with gold and silver and stainless ivory in the decoration of the palace of Menelaus, the marvellous splendour of which dazzled all beholders, and the testimony he bears to the preciousness of amber ornaments in his day is amply confirmed by the objects Dr. Schliemann recovered from the royal tombs of Mykenæ. In his interesting narrative, [2] Schliemann mentions finding in the Acropolis of Mykenæ an enormous quantity of amber beads, which " had, no doubt, been strung on thread in the form of necklaces ; " and he says :

---

[1] " Odyssey," iv. 73.

[2] " Mykenæ. A narrative of Researches and Discoveries at Mykenæ and Tiryns," by Dr. Henry Schliemann. London, 1878, pp. 214, 245.

" their presence in the tombs amongst such large treasures of golden ornaments, seems to prove that amber was considered a magnificent ornament in the time of the Mykenæan kings."

CHAPTER III.

The Mother Region—Contributions of the waves—
Popular errors—The strandhills of Samland—The
amber stratum—Distribution of amber—The amber-
tree—A Northern Atlantis—Europe under water—
The wonderful amber forest—Inclusa in amber.

AT the present day the amber of commerce is almost wholly derived from East
and West Prussia and Pomerania on the
Baltic, which have furnished it from grey
antiquity. These regions vary greatly in
productiveness, however, for although
amber nodules are found along the entire
Prussian coast-line, as they are found on
the shores of Mecklenburg, Holstein and
Denmark, on some of the islands of the

German Ocean, in Norway and Sweden, in Posen and Poland, and in Siberia as far as Kamschatka, the prolific centre—the amber-*Bildungsherd* of the North—is the rectangular peninsula of Samland, in the province of East Prussia, where shafts are sunk and mining operations carried on by the "amber kings of Königsberg," whose diving flotilla and various establishments on the coast give employment to the amphibious peasants, the descendants of the ancient Cures and Szamates. Here, too, Messrs. Stantien and Becker have set up enormous steam-dredging machines and sundry complicated contrivances, to sift from the sea-shallows the precious mineral which also is cast up by the sea on these shores—brought on the wings of the storm from occult recesses where it had long lain hidden from the eyes of men. These ejections of the sea take place with great regularity, the richest "finds" happening after the November and December storms. But from what vast repository these contributions of the waves proceed, to what geological epoch amber belongs, and how it came to be buried in the places where it is now found, are problems which long baffled the investigations of science.

Popular errors die hard. There are still people who think amber is a sea product, as there are persons who, while acknowledging its resinous nature, are of opinion that it lies in enormous masses at the bottom of the Baltic, whence it is distributed like rays, the waves bearing it to the shore according to the direction of the currents. This was a favourite notion of Dr. Berendt of Dantzig, one of the great names in amber literature. He set up the theory that, in a former geological period—at a time when Northern Germany was covered by the waters of the tertiary sea—the amber forests grew upon islands, situated just north of the present coast-line of Prussia, where the resin was amassed until, on the destruction of these islands, the accumulated amber masses were engulfed by the waves, the treasure now lying buried at the bottom of the Baltic. Other theories, from time to time, have been advanced only to disappear, and it is to the careful researches of Professor Zaddach of Königsberg into the structure of the Samland coast, that we owe almost all the knowledge of the subject we now possess.

Zaddach, whose investigations are here summarized, found that the steep strandhills of Samland, which rise in some places to a height of 180 feet, and where amber digging has been carried on for two hundred years, show three different systems or groups of layers—the top one being a stratum of diluvial marl and sand ; the middle one a bed of lignite, with light sands and grey clays ; and the lower one a layer of greensand, 50 or 60 feet in thickness, which derives its colour from innumerable grains of green earth, or glauconite. All these strata contain amber, the upper ones in isolated pieces, while the greensand layer, in its lower part, holds a stratum, 4 or 5 feet thick, of very dark earth, almost black when freshly dug, called " blue earth," or amber earth, in which amber nodules occur so abundantly that an area of 50 or 60 square rods yields several thousand pounds of the substance. This is the great amber mine of the world, and the only place in the North where the geological conditions of the mineral can be advantageously studied, as it is found nowhere else in the firm rocks in its *primary* place of deposit.

The amber of Sicily, on the contrary, is only found on or near the surface of the ground, in an accidental manner, scattered over a wide extent of country, having

been transported by down-pouring rains
and by brooks and rivers far from its
primary bed, which is believed to be in
the neighbourhood of the Central Mountains, where Gemmellaro and Maravigna,
in fact, affirmed its existence.

Zaddach's researches also threw some
light on the amber cast up by the sea on
the Samland coast, for he found that the
amber - bearing " blue earth " stratum,
which rises to different heights above the
sea-level and sinks in many places so far
below it as to be inaccessible to the miner's
shafts, also runs horizontally on a level
with the sea, where it is exposed to the
action of the waves. Further investiga-
tion has since shown that this exposed
position of the amber-stratum extends for

a distance of at least fifty miles. Here then is the source of the amber cast up by the sea. The waves constantly nibble the "blue earth," filching its golden treasure, and when lashed to fury by the storm, tear the nodules from their bed, bearing them towards the shore, mixed with seaweed and other *disjecta* of the Baltic, when the *schöpfen* or "scooping" begins, which consists in seizing the precious "amber-weed," while still floating in the sea, with long poles and nets and bearing it in triumph to the strand.[1]

---

[1] At the time of the formation and deposit of amber, Samland existed only at the bottom of the Tertiary sea, the waters of some quiet gulf or bay covering the now picturesque and interesting peninsula. Into this bay deposits of glaucous earth and

The places hitherto mentioned are the only ones which yield amber in sufficient quantities for the purposes of commerce, but small pieces are picked up in Iceland, on the east coast of England, and on the western coast of France. In the United States the mineral has been seen on Judith river, Montana, at Harrisonville, New Jersey, and on Magothy River, Maryland.

---

amber were made, and brooks and rivers from the neighbouring Northern continent brought down additional material for building up the soil, until the sea was filled up and, so to say, forced to retreat.

The greensand deposit of Samland is a marine deposit, as is proved by the fossils which exist in it, among which are vertebral bodies of fishes and sharks' teeth such as occur in *eocene* layers, and these deposits, together with the amber contained in them, belong to the *miocene* or perhaps to the *eocene*.

Single specimens, and sometimes several pieces together have been drawn by fishermen's nets in Germany out of inland lakes, ponds, and rivers, and now and then it is brought to the surface by the bubbling waters of springs. It has been observed in the brown coal of Austria and Alsace : Professor Heer discovered it in Heligoland,[1] and in small, dot-like grains, the size of a millet seed or a pea, in the coal-beds of Greenland,[2] and its presence there, he thinks, proves beyond doubt, that amber is a *miocene* formation.[3] Professor Heer

---

[1] " Flora Fossilis Arctica," pp. 7-15.

[2] The author of these pages has some splendid specimens of this Greenland coal.

[3] Professor Heer has made extended researches into the fossil vegetation of Europe, and has examined

says that amber is found in North Greenland in connection with fossil leaves in an
excellent state of preservation, and that,
as Sequoias—trees resembling the gigantic
California Redwood—are frequently met
with, it is to be supposed that they had a
part in its production.

The amber said to come from Syria,
India, and Madagascar, judging from the
specimens I have seen, is not amber at all,
but a resin nearly allied to copal, which is
the product of leaf-bearing trees growing
at the present day, while amber is the

---

collections of fossil plants obtained in Spitzbergen,
Greenland, Iceland, and Samland, which he describes
as *miocene*. Mr. J. Starkie Gardiner, Professor J. W.
Dawson, and other botanical paleontologists, however,
consider them *eocene*.

resin of acicular trees that flourished in a former geological epoch and no longer exist.

The amber-tree belongs to the flora of the Tertiary period, at the dawn of which Europe seems to have been almost in the condition of a great archipelago, some of the fairest countries we know being at that time still covered by water—the sea spreading over the south-east of England, a great part of France, Belgium, Holland, Holstein, Northern Germany, Bavaria, Hungary, and Italy. A vast continent existed in the north, however, which it is believed embraced not only the present Norway and Sweden and a large part of Russia, but extended in the arctic zone beyond Spitzbergen, where it was connected with Greenland and North America,[1] while to southward and eastward it was united with Iceland and the British Islands, dry land over a portion of the British Channel uniting England with France.

> "Where the Atlantic rolls, wide continents have
> bloomed."

---

[1] Professor W. Boyd Dawkins ("Early Man in Britain") says that through the *eocene* and *miocene* ages a continuous tract of land must have existed between Britain and America, extending northwards and westwards by way of Iceland and Greenland, while to the north-east it was continuous with Norway and Spitzbergen, offering a means of free migration for plants and animals. Professor Heer places his Atlantis more to the south-west, but both scientists agree that the existence of such a continent is the only satisfactory explanation of the presence in Europe in the Tertiary period of plants and animals the nearest allies of which belong to North America.

The southern boundary of this primeval Scandinavian continent was greatly enlarged at the close of the secondary period by deposits of the *cretaceous* sea—chalk, small grains of grey lime, glaucous marl, and far-reaching beds of greensand—and, through repeated liftings of the soil, a broad belt of land was formed which, embracing the islands of Rugen and Bornholm, extended over Jutland and the Danish islands and the whole space now occupied by the Baltic. This newly formed land was separated from Central Germany and the rest of Europe by a great sea-arm, sometimes called the North German Tertiary Sea, one of whose bays or gulfs covered East and West Prussia and Pomerania. On the borders of this northern

Atlantis, where now roll the sluggish waters of the Baltic, a rich and abundant vegetation was developed, and here, in the midst of luxuriant forests extending into the Polar area, grew the trees which produced the amber of commerce.

At the time of the formation of amber the climate, even within the arctic circle, was sub-tropical or, at any rate, warm and equable, admitting the growth in the far north of mighty forests of bald Cypress (*Taxodium*), the undoubted ancestors of the trees which lend such a weird-like charm to the marshy lands of Louisiana, Texas, and Mexico. In Spitzbergen (78° N. L.) flourished the American incense cedar (*Libocedrus decurrens*) and the deep-green Sequoia, analogous to the gigantic

Redwood (*S. Sempervirens*). This remarkable tree, which is now restricted to a
narrow district of California, grew in the
miocene period all over Europe and the
circumpolar area, together with its near
relative, the bluish-green Glyptostrobus, a
cypress now only met with in China and
Japan. In Greenland grew the large-
leafed and fragrant Magnolia, the date-
plum tree, several species of oak, pines,
poplars, and walnuts; salisburea, planera,
and the elegant Thujopsis—now only in-
digenous to Eastern Asia—while the vine,
the flowering tulip-tree, the elm, and the
mammoth-tree flourished in Iceland. It
will be seen, therefore, that in the amber-
forest plants grew side by side whose
living representatives are now scattered

far and wide through all climates from the tropics to far northern latitudes.

The amber-forest, in which a wealth of species prevailed such as has never been known since, consisted largely of coniferous trees. Professor Göppert distinguished thirty species of pines which grew in that forest, to which Menge has added one— the Taxoxylum electrochyton — and this great variety of resinous trees leads to the conclusion that amber was produced by several species of conifers; the most common tree being a "Tree of Life," closely resembling the American Thuja occidentalis, ten twigs of which, Menge says, occur in amber to one leaf or blossom of any leaf-bearing tree, and five to one of any other acicular tree. Of leaf-bearing trees, traces of which the amber has preserved for us, may be mentioned several species of oak, willows, beeches, a birch, an alder and a poplar, as well as leaves and blossoms of the camphor-tree (*cinnamomum*), whose living congeners now grow in Eastern Asia, China, and Japan.

Professor Göppert has given to the amber-pine the name of *pinites succinifer ;* and has determined no less than 163 species of plants found in amber specimens, which he has classified into 64 genera and 24 families.

The *inclusa* in amber have for us great interest ; for although, as has been pointed out, they furnish but an incomplete picture of the flora and fauna of the primeval amber-forest, " only such small animals and parts of plants—small leaflets, scales of buds, pieces of twigs, etc.,—as could be quickly surrounded by the fluid resin having been preserved," they nevertheless enable us to recognize a few features characteristic of that early epoch.   The amber-fauna is peculiar in this respect, that here are animals which rarely occur as fossils elsewhere; and many of these, which appear as mummies in the transparent resin, represent extinct forms.   As Bacon [1] says, "the Spider, Flye and Ant being tender, dissipable substances, falling into Amber, are therein buryed, finding therein both a Death, and Tombe, preserving

---

[1] " The Historie of Life and Death," p. 283.

them better from Corruption than a Royall Monument." Amongst the spiders Zaddach calls attention to the remarkable genus *Archæa*, which differs from living species by the position of the eyes, by the extraordinarily large jaws, and by the head, which is very distinctly separated from the breast.

Some of the amber-insects unite in themselves the characteristics of several families or orders now living, and present a form out of which, in the later development of the animal world, two different forms proceeded. This is illustrated by a little creature which, by the structure of its antennæ, feet, and parts of the mouth, belongs to the neuroptera, while by the scaly coverings of the forewings it reminds

us of the butterflies.   A feather, delineated
by Berendt, proves that the amber-forest
contained birds, but of mammalia nothing
has been found except a tuft of hair.
Fishes and amphibious animals are also
wanting.   Frogs, lizards, and fishes, it is
true, are shown in amber, but they have
been introduced by artificial means.
Bubbles of air and even drops of water
occur, however, and in Berendt's collection
there was a spider, in the translucent body
of which the movable air-bubble could be
seen to shift its position with every turn
given to the piece.   But Goebel's story of
a drop of water which increased in size
with the growth of the moon and de-
creased with its wane is a fable.

The amber-resin was shed in very different stages of liquidity, according to Aycke, sometimes glutinous, leaving behind it long threads, occasionally attenuated to such a degree as to preserve the delicate meshes of the cobweb, as well as the insects in it, which frequently seem to be flying with extended wings. Sometimes it fell in drops from the boughs, yielding the often-recurring drop and icicle forms; sometimes it fell on leaves lying on the ground, the forms of which it presents to us like an impression.

Many generations of trees lived and perished in the amber-forest, and enormous quantities of the resin must have been amassed, though single pieces were constantly carried away by brooks and rivers into the Tertiary sea. How the accumulated amber-masses were finally broken up, is uncertain.   But this event, it is believed, was brought about not merely by the ordinary and oft-repeated incursions of the sea into the domain of the forest, but suddenly, by some portentous cataclysm, which in a comparatively short time tore loose a great part of the resin and threw it into the Samland gulf.   It is not believed, however, that the amber-forests perished altogether at this time.   On the contrary Zaddach thinks it is probable that the production of amber belongs to several long periods in the formation of the earth, and that large masses of the resin remained buried in the soil of the higher districts until a later epoch, when the diluvial sea flooded the entire North, and with the

ruins of the devastated country scattered
the deposits far and wide. The sub-
mersion of the amber-resin was followed
by continued deposits of greensand, marl,
and other substances brought down by
brooks and rivers, piling layer upon layer
until the sea was filled up and remained so.
Samland was first laid dry and then the
rest of Prussia and the eastern part of
Pomerania, the dry land appearing like
islets, which in time were connected with
one another.

CHAPTER IV.

THE literature of the ancients is replete with speculations about amber, and around this "singular concretion" cluster delightful myths, romances and poetical fancies ; while concerning its nature, origin and habitat, the wildest and most improbable opinions have, from time to time, been entertained. But, as appears from the very ancient Heliades' myth, the Greeks, at all events, though they traced its origin to the Sun-god, knew that it was the resin of trees. It is difficult, therefore, to understand how, at a later period, when the home of amber and the methods of obtaining it were accurately known, it should have been taken for the petrified sperm or spawn of dolphins or seals; for bitumen;[1] for the product of ants or of the lynx, whence it was called *lyncurium.*

The Heliades' myth makes no reference to the locality of the Eridanus, the "beam-

---

[1] "Agricola; *de natura fossilium;*" cap. ix., pp. 479-480. The opinion of Agricola that amber is *bitumen* was adopted by almost all his contemporaries, and it was not until the beginning of this century that its true nature was established beyond controversy.

ing " river into which the sisters of Phaëthôn let fall their amber-tears, and, no
doubt, some uncertainty prevailed respecting the whereabouts of this wondrous
stream.   Herodotus does not credit the
tales concerning it, told by Greek and
Phœnician mariners, and thinks the name
was " invented " by a poet.   In modern
times various attempts have been made to
identify the Eridanus with a river in the
North or West of Europe.   The name has
been applied to the Rhine, the Rhone, and
the Vistula.   Professor Rawlinson says,
" the very name, Eridanus, lingers in the
Rhodaune, the small stream which washes
the west side of the town of Dantzig ; " but
Professor Paley agrees with Herodotus,
and regards the stream as " mythical."

The Eridanus—"the king of rivers"—is first mentioned by Hesiod;[1] and Pherecydes,[2] according to Hyginus,[3] and Æschylus, Euripides,[4] Philoxenus, Satyrus and Nicander, according to Pliny,[5] identified the Eridanus with the Padus—now called the Po—the swift-flowing, winding, and "deep-eddying" river of Northern Italy. This identification was generally accepted as conclusive by their contemporaries and by the Latins; but Pliny sneers at this

---

[1] "Theogonia," 337.

[2] Of Athens, one of the most celebrated of the early Greek logographers, who lived in the former half of the fifth century B.C.

[3] "Fabulæ, cliv. Mythog. Lat.," ed. van Staveren, 1742, 266-267.

[4] Born at Salamis, 480 B.C.

[5] "Nat. Hist." xxxvii. 11.

and other "vain statements of the Greeks," because, forsooth, in his day amber was not found on the Padus. But unless, and until it can be shown that amber never was found on the Padus, we may safely continue with Euripides to identify that river with "the ocean wave of the Adriatic shore and the waters of Eridanus, where, into the purple wave of their sire, the thrice-wretched virgins, for grief of Phaëthôn, let fall the amber-gleaming rays of their tears."[1] The fact that amber was not found on the Padus in Pliny's time does not justify the conclusion that it was not abundant there in the time of Pherecydes and Euripides. A great many

---

[1] "Hippolytus," 735-741.

errors were current amongst the Latins respecting this curious gem. It will be remembered that Diodorus of Sicily, who evidently took extraordinary pains to ascertain the home of amber, positively says it is only to be found on the island of Basilea,[1] "opposite Scythia, beyond Gallia." But, as I have shown, amber is found in Sicily, on the surface of the ground, near the place where Diodorus was born, and it was probably gathered in that neighbourhood by the Phœnicians, though, of course, it is quite possible that in the time of Diodorus the supply had temporarily ceased. The amber of Sicily is again disappearing—the "finds" dimi-

---

[1] Diodorus.

nish with every year—and, like the gold
of Ophir or the diamonds of Golconda,
this magic stone may vanish from the
sight in the localities it has rendered
famous.

Pausanias,[1] in his minute account of the
various objects of antiquity and works of
art seen by him during his travels in
Greece, mentions a statuette of the Emperor Augustus, placed in one of the
round niches of the Forum Romanum of
Trajan at Olympia, made of amber from
the sands of the Eridanus (Po) where, he
says, the substance was very rare.

Perhaps one of the most interesting
passages in ancient literature is the ac-

---

[1] "Periegesis Hel.," b. v. c. 12, § 7.

count given by Tacitus [1] of the amber-gatherers, on the shores of the tideless Baltic, where the Romans, with some reason, believed the boundaries of Nature to terminate. His narration recalls the long midsummer twilight of high northern latitudes, the surprising sunrise and cloud effects which may still be observed in that wild region; and at the same time gives a picturesque account of the Æstyan tribes and an intelligible description of the amber-diggings. But some of his statements must be taken with a grain of salt. It was not "Roman luxury" that originally gave amber a name or brought it into request; and it is difficult to believe that

---

[1] "Germania," 45.

the savages of the Baltic coast, though they offered it for sale in rude heaps without any form or polish, did not know the full value of their wares.

But however low the estimation in which this "singular concretion" was held by the rude tribes who gathered it in the distant north, it was highly prized at Rome; and Pliny[1] tells us that "the price of a figurine in amber, however small, exceeded that of a living, healthy slave." Pliny further relates that the Emperor Nero bestowed the appellation amber on his beloved Poppea's hair, from which it has been inferred that this fair creature was a blonde, with golden locks.

---

[1] XXXVII. 12.

He also mentions that, at the beginning of Nero's reign, the demand for amber was so great that to obtain a supply for the gladiatorial exhibitions, a Roman knight was sent to the north by the commercial road, who brought back to Rome an enormous quantity, including a lump weighing thirteen pounds. According to Solinus ("Polyhist.," ch. xx.), this knight returned with thirteen thousand pounds of amber, which a German king sent as a present to the emperor. With this glittering gem the circus was adorned with ostentatious splendour; and the gladiators, who defiled before the emperor with the greeting, "*Ave Cæsar, morituri te salutant*," wore it as an amulet or charm on the breast to insure them victory.

Amongst the Romans, amber held its place as an object of luxury, notwithstanding the importation of large quantities of precious stones from the East. In the Homeric age the fair Greeks seem to have known that this was a gem peculiarly becoming to their complexions, but the resources of the Greek dames were limited, while the Roman ladies had diamonds, rubies, and sapphires, gems unknown in the Mediterranean countries until after the invasion of India by Alexander the Great.[1]

---

[1] Many articles in constant use are of recent introduction. Even the *fork*, the emblem *par excellence* of modern refinement, was not employed in Europe until the seventeenth century, although it had long been in use amongst the Fijians, and, in fact, belongs

The ancients employed amber as a
medicine, and it is still prescribed by
physicians in France, Germany, and Italy,
and several chemists in Paris keep it constantly in stock. It has been worn by
ladies and children from time immemorial as an amulet, sometimes carved
into amphoræ, and has been pronounced
of service, either taken internally or worn
round the neck.[1] It has always been re-

---

to the Second Stone Age, to which remote period
we are also indebted for most of our cereals, for that
refreshing beverage *beer*, and for that most delicious
bivalve, the *oyster* "on the half shell," which has
descended to us in a direct line from the *Kjökken-
moddings*, or shell-mounds of the Danish coast.

[1] Callistratus gave the name of *Chryselektron* to
amber of a clear golden colour, which, worn round
the neck, cured ague; ground up with honey and

garded as a "lucky stone," protecting the wearer against the influence of the "evil eye ; " and there are scholars who see in this supposititious quality the root of *elektron*, the Greek name for amber, the verb ἀλέξω, *alexo*, signifying "to ward off, to protect."

Sir Thomas Browne in his "Urn Burial" mentions, on the authority of "Vigeneri," an elephant of amber as amongst the contents of a Roman urn belonging to Cardinal Farnese.   I have looked into "Vigeneri,"

---

rose oil it was a specific for deafness, and with attic honey for dimness of sight.   Dioscorides thought highly of amber as a medicine and Aurifaber, in his "Historia Succini," has furnished numerous receipts for its use.   "I am not ashamed to say that I have tried it," he says, "and it has not been in vain."

otherwise M. Blaise de Vigenère, an
eminent French savant, who lived from
1523 to 1596, and spent several years in
Rome, where his name got Italianised.
His account of the contents of this Roman
urn is so like the catalogue of a conjurer's
bag, that I have taken pains to translate
just what he says. It will be observed
that, besides the "elephant," Vigenère
mentions four other objects sculptured in
amber ;—*i.e.*, a Cupid, a Venus, a sleeping
Cupid, and a figure of Silence—as part of
the contents of this funereal vessel. His
account is highly entertaining and may be
found, in good, old-fashioned French, in
"Annotations sur Tite Live," p. 868, as
follows :

" In the year 1565 there was found in a

little garden of the church of St. Blasius
at the foot of St. Peter's *ad vincula* in
Rome a funereal urn or vase, containing
the following objects, most of which I saw
in the cabinet of Cardinal Farnese in the
following year :—a Faustina of cassidonium
(calcedony) with pedestal of the same :
a Roman boundary stone : a nude goddess
of agate : another smaller one, with bases
of the same : a Mercury also of agate : a
Cupid of yellow amber : a Venus and a
sleeping Cupid of the same material, and a
figure of Silence, holding a finger from his
chin to his nose : a large head of Jupiter
with bust of agate : another smaller one
and still another, with a base, all of agate :
a small Jupiter, a Venus, two nude god-
desses and a Mars of cassidonium ; a

Jupiter with bust of lapis lazuli: a very fine Domitian; another smaller one; a Trajan; a figure of Silence of agate: two figurines of crystal: two heads; an ape; a head of Alexander the Great; one of Socrates; two others unknown—all of cassidonium: a head engraved on crystal, the upper part forming a shield: a mask of jasper: a larger one; two smaller ones, like children's, and a tiger sucking his foot —all of cassidonium: a lion of jet: an eagle on a ball of agate: a small elephant of amber: a little dog of cassidonium gnawing a bone: a vase; five smaller ones and a glass of agate; a spoon of cassidonium: a twig of white coral: two big apples of crystal: another smaller one: a club of Hercules; a branch of a tree; a grasshopper (*une cigale*);[1] a finger of natural size; a vase with a cover; a cup; three glasses; two spoons; a little basket; six

---

[1] It has been averred that the ancients did not sculpture the grasshopper. But the grasshopper, or the *cicada*—an insect so closely resembling the grasshopper as to render it impossible in art objects to detect the difference—may be observed on early Greek coins, notably those of Metapontum and Akragas, and is delineated on antique gems (*intagli*), on sundry Greek vases, and on a Pompeian wall, where it appears as an accessory in a *genre* picture; and both the grasshopper and cicada are frequently mentioned in ancient literature. The poets, indeed, never tired of singing the praises of "the clear-sounding cicada, whose meat and drink is the life-giving dew."—("Hesiod. S. Herculis," 393.) But, as an object by itself, this animal—whether grass-hopper or cicada—is certainly very rare. There is one in rock crystal in Berlin, and Mr. A. S. Murray, Keeper of Greek and Roman Antiquities in the British Museum, has kindly called my attention to

hazel-nuts and a large ring with a Victory engraved on it—all of rock crystal. What a curious fancy to bury all this with one!"

Curious indeed! But the ancients regarded the matter from another standpoint, and buried with their dead the things dear to them in life—their ornaments, weapons, implements, gauds, etc.—and in this way many rare and precious objects

---

the existence, in his department, of one in bronze, said to have been found in Rhodes, and to another in terra-cotta. The golden *cicadæ* mentioned by Thucydides (i. 6) and Aristophanes (*Knights*, 1331) as having been employed by the Athenians and Ionians as hairclasps, were, according to Helbig ("Das Homerische Epos," pp. 242-246), simply metal spirals, like those found in Italo-Greek tombs, called *cicadæ* from a fancied resemblance between metallic spiral rings and the body rings of the animal.

are preserved which otherwise would have been wholly lost.

Juvenal describes his wealthy patron as drinking at his banquets from a bowl embossed with beryls and relievi in amber; and Heliodorus styles the fibula on the mantle of Theagenes a " Pallas carved out of amber."

Martial has some charming epigrams, upon a viper, upon an ant, and upon a bee imprisoned in amber, and he repeatedly compares the delicious fragrance of the substance with the fragrance of a kiss.[1]

Shakespeare mentions amber in " Love's Labour's Lost" and in " The Taming of

---

[1] Martial, iii. 65 ; v. 37 ; xv. 8.

the Shrew." When Petruchio promises to take Katherine on a visit to her father, he says, she shall go furnished

"With scarfs and fans and double change of bravery,
With amber bracelets, beads and all this knavery."

Several passages in the Bible have been supposed to refer to amber, and the Biblical Gan-Eden, or Garden of Eden,— the cradle of the human race, the primitive abode of man,—has been described as situated in the amber-land,

". . . the land of the pine-trees—"

the Baltic being the River Pison, and the Tree of Life the amber tree, the fairest and most important in the world.

This startling theory was advanced nearly a century ago, in 1799, by Johann

Gottfried Hasse,[1] a scholar of Königsberg; and since his day the researches of Heer, Saporta, Hooker, Gray, Wallace, and other prominent paleontologists have shown that the circumpolar area—the lost *miocene* continent in the north—was the mother region that gave birth to a great variety of plants and animals from which the life-forms now existent in lower latitudes have proceeded. M. le Marquis de Saporta [2] says: "We are inclined to remove to the circumpolar

---

[1] "Preussen's Ansprüche als Bernsteinland das Paradies der Alten und Urland der Menschheit gewesen zu sein." Von Dr. Johann Gottfried Hasse, Consistorialrath und Professor zu Königsberg. Königsberg, 1799.

[1] "Un Essai de Synthèse Paléoethnique," par M. le Marquis G. de Saporta. "Revue des Deux Mondes." Livraison du 1er Mai, 1883.

regions of the North the probable cradle
of primitive humanity. From there only
could it have radiated as from a centre, to
spread into the several continents at once,
and to give rise to successive emigrations
towards the South. This theory best
agrees with the presumed march of the
human races. . . . It is equally in accord
with the most authentic and most recent
geological data, and, besides man, it is
applicable to the plants and animals which
accompanied him, and which have continued to be most closely associated with
him in the temperate regions, which after-
wards became the seat of his civilizing
power."

When the North Pole shall have finally
been reached, and its fossil remains

thoroughly explored, additional evidence in support of the theory will doubtless come into view, and the original and ingenious proposition of Buffon (" Epoques de la Nature ") that life first appeared in the northern circumpolar area of the globe, be sustained.   In the meantime the great lone-land of the North presents an ample field for the roaming instincts of speculation and imagination ;   but, when the secrets entombed in rock and ice come to be unveiled, the Baltic may have to give place to a yet more northern clime as the primal home of " the Tree of Life."

CHISWICK PRESS :—CHARLES WHITTINGHAM AND CO.
TOOKS COURT, CHANCERY LANE, LONDON.

www.ingramcontent.com/pod-product-compliance
Lightning Source LLC
Chambersburg PA
CBHW020758020726
47495CB00008B/2497